D1177494

“So, Jerry… You make cookies too?”
“You bet!”

“You’re
gonna get it,
Jerry!”

"Juuuust kidding!"
Ha!
Ha!
Ha!
Ha!
Ha!
Ha!
Ooooof!

"Don't worry. Gobble-Fangs takes over on Monday. He's a handful. Just what you wanted."

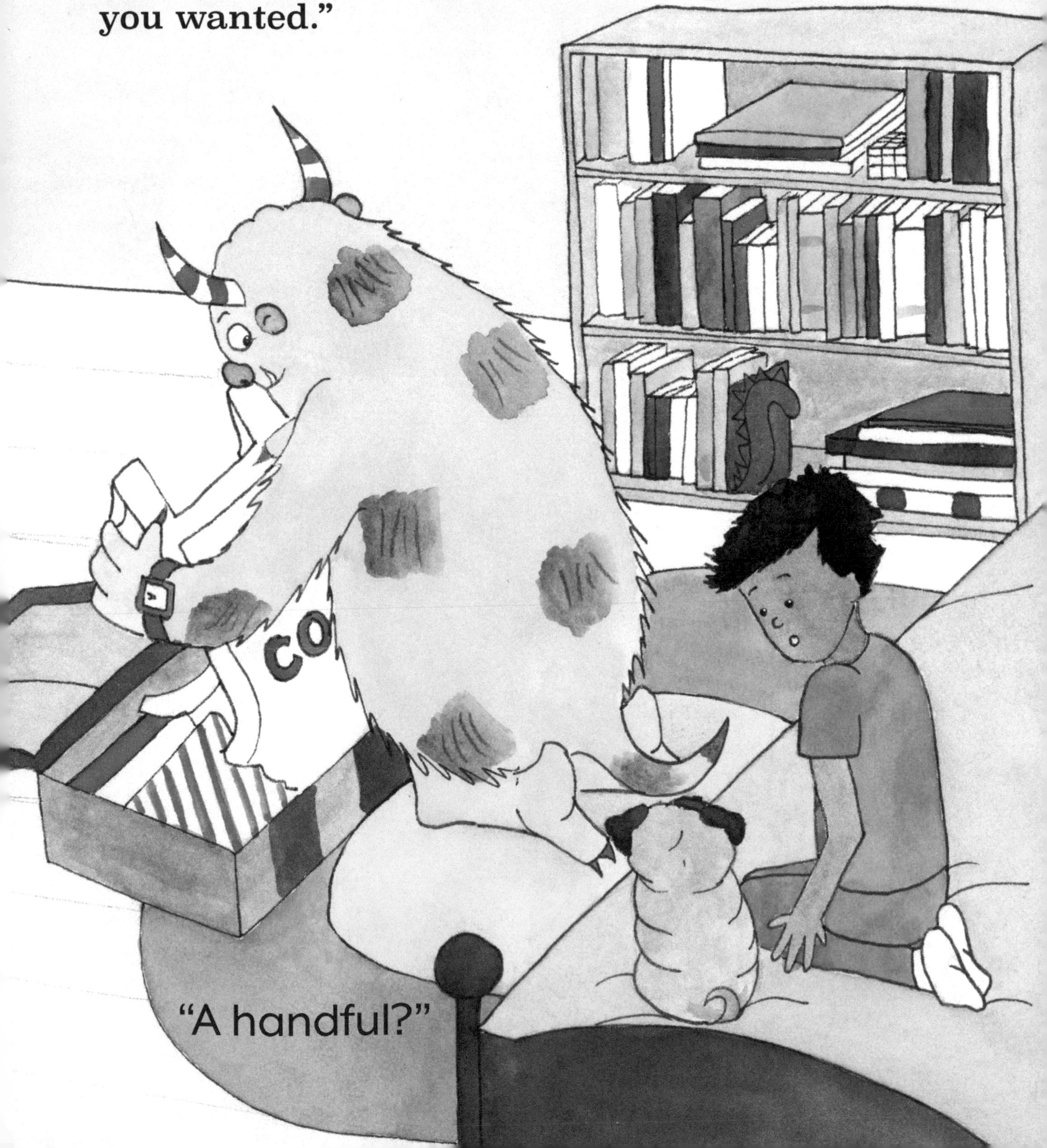

"A handful?"

“You’re **leaving?!**

But you **just** started!”

“You want to bake
for me all day?”

“I’d love to…

**but did
I mention
I’m only
a temp?”**

"That was **amazing**, Jerry!"

"Thanks! You made me
think about the things I enjoy.
It turns out, I **love** to bake!
I could do it all day!"

"Well, it **does** smell really good." I took a bite.

And **another**... And **another**...

Until I was licking my plate.

Lasagna?

"Sprinkle-
cheese on top?"

I rubbed my eyes.
"What time is it?"

**"It's
middle-of-the-night
snack time!"**

"And thumb wrestling...

And spitting watermelon seeds...

And..."

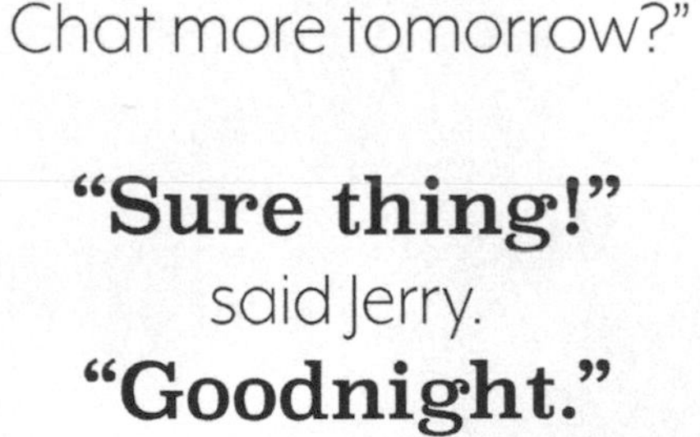

"**Whoa,** Jerry.
That's a fun list, but I'm exhausted.
Chat more tomorrow?"

"Sure thing!"
said Jerry.
"Goodnight."

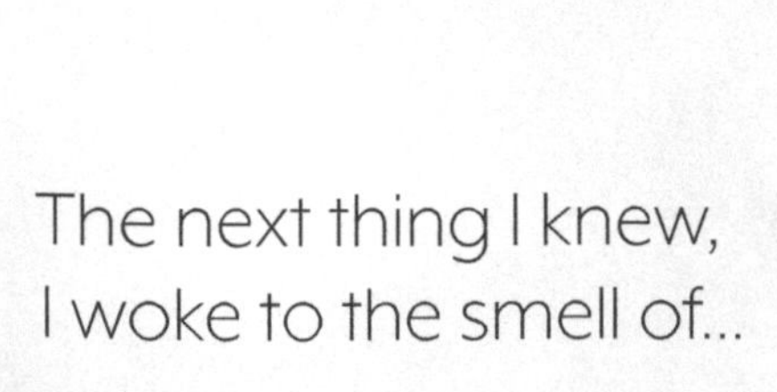

The next thing I knew,
I woke to the smell of...

"And I like
painting rocks..."
"And giving
pedicures..."

"I like making waffles."
My stomach growled.
"What else?"
"I like giving hugs!"
"Well, you **are** really good at them."

"Jerry... you **know**
you're not scary... **Right?**"
(I had to make sure he knew this)
"I know.
I wish I were a natural
like my brother, Hank.
He was **born** scary."
"What were
you born to do, Jerry?"

Jerry slumped over.

"I'm sorry I raised my voice at you."

"It's OK. I just thought maybe you would enjoy something else more."

"More than being a monster?

I'll always be a monster.

But maybe I don't have to be a scary monster?"

“Of course I do!

I’m a monster!”

I finally said,
"You don't really like this
'being scary'
stuff, do you?"

I wanted to laugh.
I chewed my nails instead.

Jerry nibbled on
his claws.

Then, he straightened
my books...

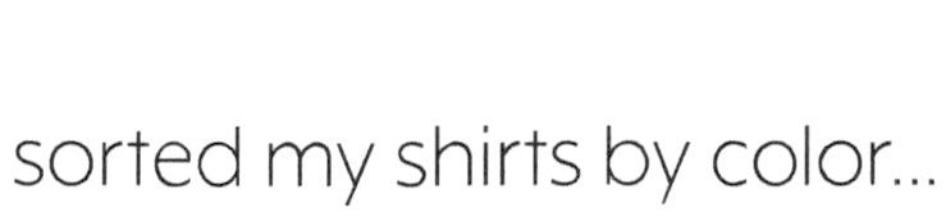

sorted my shirts by color...

and cleaned my mirror
with his monster breath.

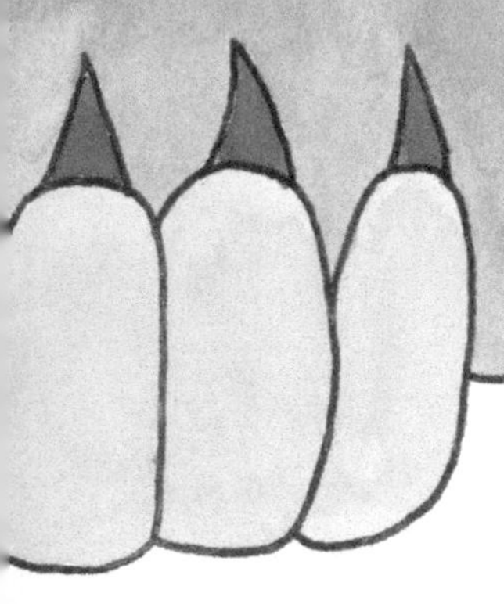

"It's **really** dark under there...
and a bit of a tight squeeze."

"How about you crawl under my bed
and claw at my sheets?" I said.

Jerry peeked under the bed.

Jerry opened his mouth, *carefully.*

"**Ew!** You slimed my pillow!"

"Oops. Sorry. Overactive salivary glands."

"Let me guess. It runs in the family?"

Jerry nodded.

Jerry opened wide.

Then **wider.**

Until...

POP!

"Ouch!"

he whimpered.

"I have this jaw thing. It runs in the family."

"Um. OK. Maybe don't open so wide next time?"

"Good advice."

"You're a **ghost** now?"
"I'm just warming up!"
"Why don't you scare me with your big pointy teeth then?"

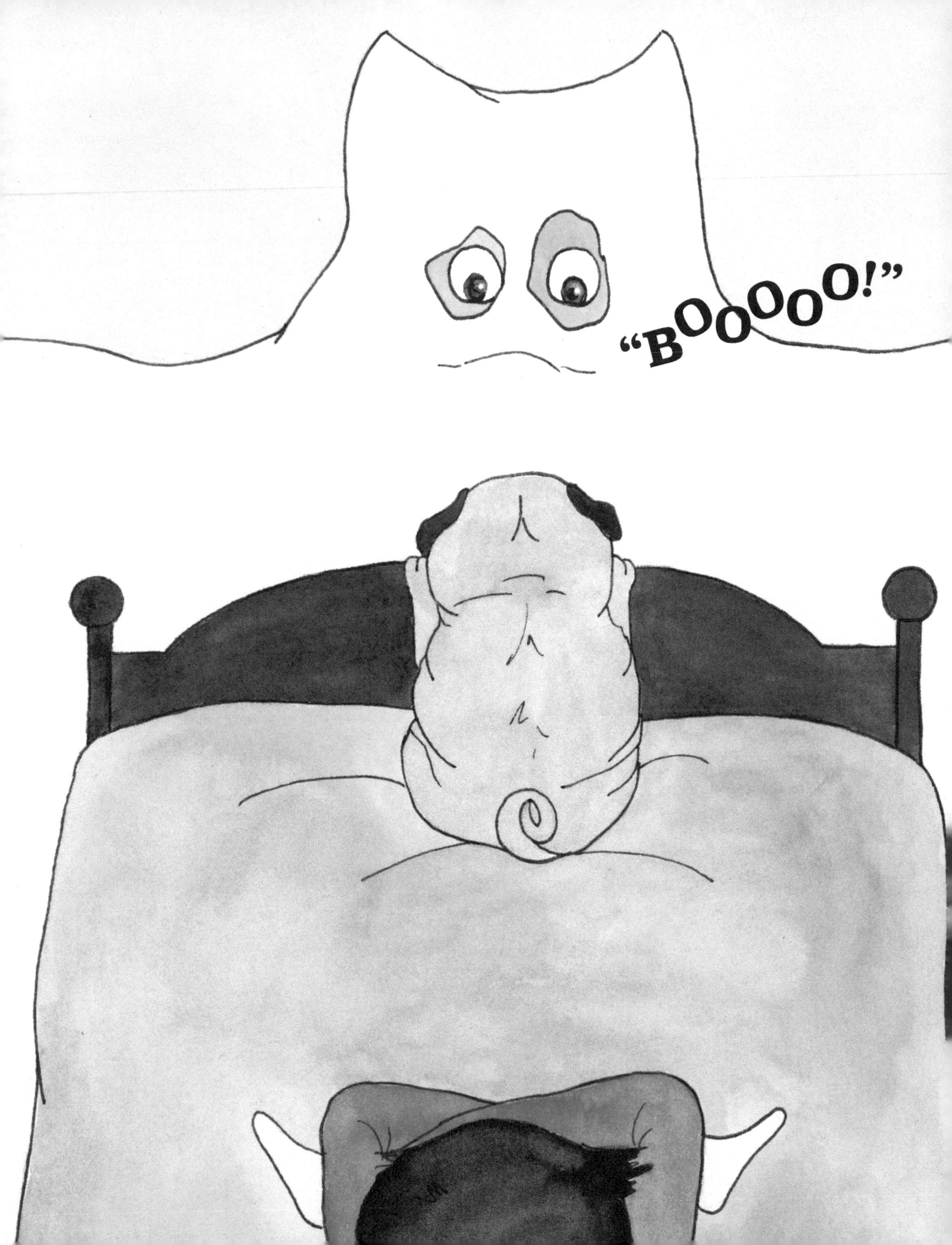
"BOOOOO!"

"Scary monsters
don't hug,"
I said.

(but I hugged
him anyway)

"Soooooooo...
do you want to
try scaring me?"

**"OK.
Close
your eyes
and count
to five."**

"One...

Two...

Three...

Four...

Five!"

Jerry is my current monster. When we met, he said,

"Hi, I'm Jerry. Call me **Scary** Jerry, if you like.

Wanna hug?"

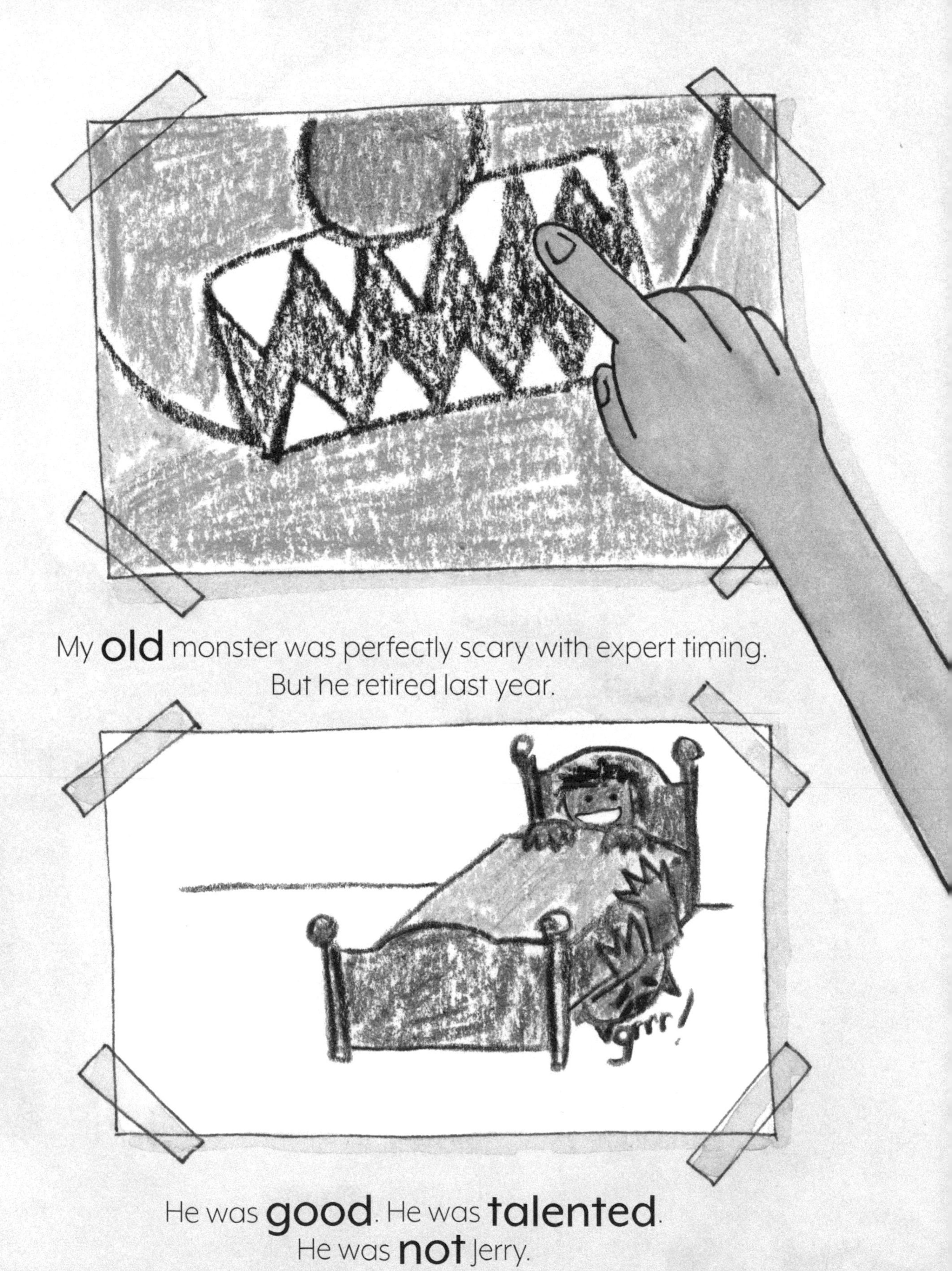

My **old** monster was perfectly scary with expert timing.
But he retired last year.

He was **good**. He was **talented**.
He was **not** Jerry.

MY OLD MONSTER

MY old MONSTeR

To the cuties who most inspire my writing (and who are not allowed to grow up)
— Shane, Aaron, Summer, and Micah.
To Scott, my loving hubs, whose ideas help guide me in the right direction.
To my mom, just because.
To Caryn, who brought this ol' Jerry monster to life.
I am forever grateful to you all! – *SK*

To the boy who loved hot pink, grew up to wear a hot pink watch, believes in me
more than I do, & never grimaces at my book obsession.
To my little girls who redefine princesses & monsters for me every day.
And to Shelley, who started this whole thing & brought me along for the ride. – *CS*

Not So Scary Jerry Copyright © 2017
Artwork Copyright © 2017 By Caryn Schafer
All rights reserved. No part of this book may be reproduced in any form
or by any electronic or mechanical means including information storage and retrieval systems
– except in the case of brief quotations embodied in critical articles or reviews –
without permission in writing from its publisher:
Clear Fork Publishing, P.O. Box 870, 102 S. Swenson, Stamford, Texas 79553 · (325)773-5550

Summary: Monsters don't hug. Or do they? With a little coaching,
can a friendly monster learn to be mean and scary? Through fun and quirky dialogue,
Boy and Monster discover a lot about each other, but perhaps even more about oneself.
A delicious story of friendship and self-acceptance with hilarious twists and turns along the way.

Printed and Bound in the United States of America.
ISBN - 978-1-946101-32-7 · LCN - 2017950769

www.clearforkpublishing.com

Kinder, Shelley,
Not so scary Jerry /
[2017]
33305240783070
sa 05/09/18

NOT SO SCARY JERRY

written by
Shelley Kinder

illustrated by
Caryn Schafer

"I think this is the beginning
of a **delicious** friendship,"
I said.

And it was.

MY JERRY
MONSTER

Shelley Kinder

author

Shelley lives in Indiana with her not-so-scary husband and their four little monsters. When Shelley is not writing or cleaning up after monsters, she's probably thinking about writing (or about how she should be cleaning). Shelley has known from a young age that she wanted to write children's books, but she insisted on going to college for unrelated things. She vows not to get sidetracked again. *Not So Scary Jerry* is Shelley's first picture book. Visit her at www.shelleykinder.com.

Caryn's absolutely favorite color is green. She thinks it may be from her childhood blanket which is an oddly similar shade of green to Jerry. That wasn't intentional... she thinks. She does still have that blanket and it makes fantastic forts, something she loves to do with her kids. Caryn also loves to bake, take pictures, and talk about books. Caryn really loves books. She would rather choose a favorite star than pick a favorite book. She began drawing and making books when she was a little kid. Caryn studied art in school, worked for several years as a graphic designer, and is now pursuing her passion for picture books in every spare moment. She lives in New York City with her husband and two daughters. *Not So Scary Jerry* is her first picture book. Her art, book reviews, photos, and sketches can be found at smellingoranges.com.

Caryn Schafer
illustrator

CPSIA information can be obtained
at www.ICGtesting.com
Printed in the USA
LVHW07*0019060418
572526LV00017B/83/P